WICCA ON A FULL MOON

BOOK I

THE JOURNEY THROUGH THE FOREST

WRITTEN BY SUSAN CHRISTINE SLATER

ISBN: 978-0-578-01850-8

Publisher: WWW.LULU.COM

Author: Susan Slater

Copyright: ©April 2009

By Susan Christine Slater

Standard Copyright License

Language: English

Country: United States

Edition: first Edition

BOOK 1: JOURNEY THROUGH THE FOREST

"Perception is the key to reality"

A story of: Melinda Fairling of Foothill Forest, Ireland

Book Description:

The little village of Hill dale, in the Foothill Forest of Ireland holds many secrets. Magic is not uncommon. Actually, most of the villagers have one or more powers that they wield freely. Although Melinda Fairling has never been able to master any powers of her own, she still has hope that she will have a magical future. This, the first story of Melinda Fairling, is one of a great journey to find her home, family, and magic of her own. Since she was three years old, Melinda has lived in the village of Hill Dale after being separated from her mother deep within the forest on all Hallows Eve, Her birthday. Melinda never knew the truth of her parentage until her thirty-third birthday. She was most surprised! The truth of her past has led

Melinda on a long and tediousness journey to find her mother,

and to learn of her magic abilities that have arrived so suddenly.

What will Melinda find at the end of her Journey? Just read and

see...

Journey to Fairyland
: By Joannda Riche

You must believe with all your heart and soul.
Let no man tell you otherwise,
Or fill your head with darkened lies.

The way to get there is many in choice,
But a good first step is the inner voice.
By air, or water, by earth or fire,
Fairyland is your heart's desire.

There you are free, all you can be,
And everything is real.
You could sit for a while,
Upon a sundial,
And chase the rays of the light,
You could float on the air,
Without any care,
Or fly with butterfly wings.
Buzz with the bees, and fly through the trees,
Float down with the falling leaves.

You could go on a boat,
Through sparkling waters,
Made out of the shell of a tortoise.
Sit in the ring where the fairies all sing,
Drink, dance, fairy fling.
Diddle on the fiddle, play fairy in the middle,
Sparkle, shine, and drink buttercup wine.
T'is not far, you must believe,
Just follow the voice from within.

Chapter 1

"The beginning"

Dear Diary:

Hello, my name is Melinda
Fairling. I live in a small village in the
middle of Foothill Forest. The village is
named Hill Dale. Everyone has magic and
uses it freely. My powers are yet to
develop fully. Although I have no set
power, I am useful with medicine and
tentures.

I turn thirty-three on this,
the most magical night of the Wiccan
calendar. This is All Hallows Eve! I

am so happy to have this to be my date of being birthed!

The moon is so full and bright that I will need no lantern to see where I am going as I leave the village to collect a special mushroom called the bioluminescent mushroom. This special mushroom glows in the dark. I want to collect these for our all hallows eve celebration and ceremonies' tonight. We use the mushrooms to cast protection spells for the village. These are very magical mushrooms. These mushrooms rest at the base of the white oak trees in the forest. You can only find it at night, they are easier to find during a full moon. These mushrooms glow the most wonderful colors of purple and green that any mundane human has ever seen! The moonlight helps them to glow brighter.

While out on the hunt for mushrooms, I heard the oddest story about myself. I will not pretend that I have not felt it, and I will be the first to tell you, I always had a sneaking feeling that I was an outsider in Hill Dale. However, I did not know that for sure until now. Tonight I found out that I was possibly from outside of the forest. This saddened and surprised me to be sure. I did not want to be right. However, as far as my powers go, I never really seemed to share any of the other villagers' powers. At least, I suspected before tonight that I had no real powers of my own. Oh, boy was I wrong! I was amazed and deeply distraught to hear what I heard..........Listen to this...

Many years earlier:

Anna Bess was a, very adventurous and beautiful, young woman of sixteen years old. She lived with her mother, Rose, and her grandmother, Trisha Ellie. They lived in the village of Hill Dale of the Foothill Forest, in Ireland. She had straight tri-colored brunet hair that was well kept. She had exquisite blue eyes that sparkled and shined like none others'. Anna Bess was by far the smallest woman of her age in the whole village, being only 5 foot 3 inches tall. She was always wondering around the woods looking for adventure. She usually stayed close to home except for once or maybe twice. She was always bringing home some sort of ill fallen animal or another. Anna Bess was a natural healer; she could heal anything or anyone. Her powers of healing were greater than her grandmothers'. Usually she never even had to use magic spells or incantations. She only had to think about the ending result that she wanted and it was so.

One of her best friends was a young man named Henrie. He was a tall, dark haired, dark eyed boy that every girl in the village always doted on. Although He was three years older than Anna Bess, and could have any girl of his choosing, He was well smitten with her. He ran around the forest with her, just, to make sure of her safety. At least this was his answer when anyone asked.

One night when there was a full moon, they were out and about on the hunt for the bioluminescent mushroom when they found a little girl sitting under a tree, she was glowing with the fireflies. Both were highly stunned and shocked to see this. Henrie went to search around in the area for her parents, because no young child this small could have gotten here alone. He found some footprints, only they led into the nearby creek and was not able to be followed from there. Both of them spent hours calling out into the forest for anyone who could hear them, no one answered. They decided to get their mushrooms and take the child to the village council. Anna Bess was allowed to question the child. She found out that the she was three, and her name was told to be Melinda Fairling. She had told Anna Bess her mommy left her their while she went to look for food. This gave the village elders and trackers a place to start at, as far as looking for her missing parents. Rose allowed her daughter to take charge little Melinda and to give her a home until her parents or other family could be located. Everyone searched although no one could locate Melinda's family. Almost a year passed without anyone claiming her. Melinda was not from the village and no one had ever heard of a family in the forest named Fairling. Could this mean that she was not from the forest? Perhaps her name was not Fairling. Anna Bess decided to raise her as her own, after not being able to locate the Fairling family. Melinda was never told of these events in her life.

Anna Bess, Rose and Trisha Ellie were sad for the child, however, they did not treat her any different than any other village child. She was well cared for and was taught the survival skills that any good witch or Elvin child should know. By age six, Melinda knew every plant and animal species that resided in their land. Melinda was taught to read and write, and she was taught about magic. She was very good at the healing as well as other spells until she turned ten. This is when she became unable to do magic of any kind. She would practice as taught; she just could not get it to work.

Anna Bess's grandmother passed to the heavens when Melinda was just eleven and because of Trisha Ellie's death, Melinda took on more responsibilities in the village.

She was now the local witch that all came to for their herbs and tentures and other natural remedies and cures. Melinda had always been an agreeable sort of child, as well as a quick learner. She never really caused any trouble, though she was a bit like Anna Bess, in respect to the fact that she enjoyed wandering around in the forest all alone. She loved to wander out into the forest and collect her rare herbs and flowers and vines for her remedies and tentures.

Anna Bess was eventually married to Henrie and had two girls of her own, Kelsey and Danielle. When their first and only son, Nighgiel, was three, she passed to the Heavens. It was a sad day for all because Anna Bess was well liked by all of the villagers, most of whom she grew up with. Melinda was sixteen when Anna Bess passed. Melinda seemed to be proud to help with the raising of Anna Bess's other Children as well as caring for Henrie. Though she was happy, when she turned twenty-one, she longed to have a husband and children of her own. She always believed that Anna Bess and Henrie were her true parents, until the night of her thirty-third birthday.

Now it is all hallows eve, 30 years later, and it is Melinda's thirty-third Birthday. She played a critical part in the opening ceremony that was to be held later in the night. The females in her family had always headed up the prayers' and she was no different. She thought that it would be great to have some Bioluminescent, Glow in the dark mushrooms from the forest. She knew that there was just enough time to go on the hunt for some. Tonight There was a full moon, which made the hunt all the easier.

As Melinda reached the side of a slow moving, shallow, Creek that ran some distance from her home, she noticed a few women moving through the trees. She stopped to watch them. She did this to identify them before approaching them in the dark.

There were people living in the forest that were not part of her nearby village. No one knew them so, just to be careful, Melinda stooped down beside the creek and watched them. They were moving slowly across the creek, away from her. Melinda noticed that one of the women was wearing a dress that she herself had made only a month or so ago. This was her grandmother Rose and her cousins, Tia and Belladonna! *Tia is a warm-hearted young woman of twenty-eight. She has auburn red hair that is quite wavy. Her lovely hair falls to her waist. She has the most brilliant, sky blue, eyes. She is of medium build and quite muscular for a woman of 5'8" tall. I am very small comparatively speaking, myself being only 4'3" tall. Now, Belladonna, being quite the opposite of Tia, was twenty years old and only 5'4". She was a kitchen witch and showed it well by her plumpness.*

She has a short straight haircut that is very elfish in style. She has dark brown eyes with golden specs and a black ring encircles the brown. I believe them both to be very lovely women indeed.

Melinda stood and started to walk towards the women when she heard her grandmother speaking in a hushed voice to her cousins. Melinda could not make out what was being said, though she could feel it was a secret. Therefore, she moved closer to a group of white oak trees that her Grandma Rose and her cousins were standing by. Melinda then heard a story that her grandmother had never told in her presence before.......

Grandmother Rose said, "Melinda was found in this very part of the forest thirty years ago tonight by my daughter, Anna Bess. Melinda was sitting beneath this white oak tree, playing with a group of lightning bugs. This was not extraordinary in its self for a child of her age; however, Melinda was also glowing along with the lightning bugs! This was shocking because there was none in our village with this power! This power was completely unheard of before that night. Anna Bess brought this small child, Melinda, home. She tried for months to find her parents, to no avail. No one from our village had ever been to the other side of the great forest and never had a reason to venture that far from home. We searched the forest for any with the name Fairling; none could even imagine where such a small child could have come from. Melinda had the most glorious blond hair; it seemed to glow with the sun's rays. She had the most unusual green eyes that had never been seen in the Village of Hill Dale before. Now that Melinda is Thirty three, I fear that she will start to come into her powers that she has long ago forgotten and I just don't know what to do." Rose said. "So girls, *what are we to do?"*

Tia and Belladonna were quite shocked. They really did not have any ideas. Tia suggested that they send Melinda away through the forest with a party of men to locate her original family and find out about her wonderful power of glowing. However, they could not send her alone and they could think of no one to send with her as Tia had suggested. They were unable to come up with a way to explain to her that she did not belong to their village. They felt the news would be hurtful any which way she heard it. They all agreed that she should hear it from her grandmother Rose.

When Melinda heard the conversation, she was torn between leaving the village to search on her own, or making her presence known to her family from behind the trees.

Chapter 2

"All Hallows Eve, Magic reborn"

"I feel so distraught listening to my grandmother's story. I always knew that I was different than all the other villagers; I just never thought I was from elsewhere thru the forest! However, I guess it all makes perfect sense! I have blond hair and all the other villagers have red or brunet hair. I have green eyes, no one else does. I am quite short for the village; all the women are about five and a half feet tall and the men around six feet tall. I am just 4 feet 3 inches. Everyone in Hill Dale has powers and can cast spells. I have never developed in that way. I can brew medicine and grow wonderful herbs however; I never knew that I had a rare and unknown power! I cannot seem to get spells spoken aloud or otherwise to ever work correctly for me. Something always goes wrong or just…not right! I wish my grandma had told me. It seems to me that I should have been told long before now. I cannot imagine why they would even be discussing sending me away! I have not done anything, and I have never even been told of my being found, or lost for that matter. I may have glowed once, although I have never glowed, as I have gotten older. I am definitely in shock! I decided to sit down behind the trees to think it over."

GUESS what I finally found!? Right there behind that very tree, the glow in the dark mushrooms! I was so thrilled that I squealed out in glee! Yes, I forgot all about the story I had just heard, for the moment anyway. My grandmother Rose darted around the trees to find out what the noise was. When Rose, Tia, and Belladonna saw me sitting on the ground they forgot their talk and focused on me. Tia asked, *"Is everything well?"* I answered, *"Yes, it's splendid! Look what I found!"*

Belladonna fell to her knees on the ground in front of me. She was inspecting my find, when all of a sudden; she started looking at me, as did Tia and Grandma Rose. They were staring at me! I kept asking *"What?"* what is wrong? *Would someone speak to me, please!"* No one would answer me. I finally said, in an overconfident voice, *" Fine, I will take these back to the village for the ceremonies tonight."* Grandma Rose said" *No child, Look in the water! Melinda, go over there, look in the stream! Hurry now, GO, GO!"* I was a little frightened of their stares and her words. I crawled over to the creek; I looked down into the water...My green eyes were glowing in the dark along with the Green mushrooms; the same exact color! I was in awe too! I asked, "Grandmother, What is happening to me? Why are my eyes glowing like this?"

৪৩

Grandmother rose felt it was now time to tell me the story. I only sat and listened. When she was done, I said, *"Where could I possibly be from? Was I abandoned? Was I Lost? I guess I could always go look for where I came from. Would my true family accept me? I would rather live out my days here* among my great friends and my family if you will still have me. I feel that if I was wanted by my family they would have looked for me to no end." Tia answered me with, *"I feel that you should find out who you are before you settle down and marry. You know neither where you are from nor who your true family is. You also do not know why you were out in the forest all alone. You may have been left here in hopes that someone would find and care for you, and to keep you from danger."* She sighed, and then continued with *"We must form a party and go to the other side of the great forest in search of your people. I know a few men who might be willing to help for little or no pay. I also know a great forest tracker. We must venture out by morning so that we may find out the truth behind your being left in the forest... It is a necessary part of life to know where you belong as well as where you come from... I shall go with you as your friend, family, and guide. Please, let us venture home to the celebrations and ceremonies for tonight. Then we shall rest and leave in the morning."* I said, with renewed voice, *"Let us go!" I too am eager to know my past as well as find my Family............*

We all walked, together, back to the village. This is where I experienced another strange, however   wonderful,   power…

Chapter 3

"The Ceremony"

Grandmother Rose insisted that we go to the village center right away where we could prepare for the all hallows eve ceremony. We had to charge our athemes and stones. We had to cut our herbs and flowers. We had to light all the candles and torches. We also had to bring out our personal alter supplies. We have in the past; found it was easier to cast our protection circles before the ceremonies' rather than at the beginning of them. The ceremonies' would consume too much time otherwise.

I cut my herbs and charged my stones. I laid out all my items on my personal alter and proceeded with my special tasks. As I set out to light all the candles and all the torches surrounding the magical circle, I experienced the oddest thing. As I lit a torch, I seemed to absorb the light and I started to glow faintly! I lit another and another until I was glowing brighter than all the torches together! I felt the warm glow. It was not uncomfortable; it was not as if I was on fire, though I did shine as bright as any fire I had ever seen! Every one of the female villagers that were there to help with the preparations had stopped to watch what would happen next. No one seemed frightened; they were just all in awe. I was certainly startled to say the least. Now it seemed that my eyes were glowing green and my whole body was glowing a brilliant white. I was half expecting to float away before the night was over! Even with as startled as I was, I continued with my tasks at hand. Lighting all the candles was next on my list. I found that I did not seem to glow brighter with every candle I lit. I only got so bright, and then stayed that bright. I was in love with these powers, though they were all so new to me! I could only wonder what else I could do. I continued with my tasks and started to cast the circle around our ceremony area. As I cast the circle, it started to shimmer a golden color. I was beginning to wonder if my parents were of the Fae Folk, certainly they were not. I have no wings even if I am smaller than all of the other villagers. Not really a realistic thought, because the Fae Folk are tiny and they fly, I did have the fleeting thought however! Fairies glow do they not? I had always heard that they did... I guess that I was most amazed that my spell cast for the circle was actually working! I asked my grandmother to assist me with the last task I had. I was to say the blessing of the village. I *had* to find another to take my place. I just had to! The blessing is to protect the village and its entire people. I was afraid to be at the main alter in front of the whole village. I was afraid as well, what might happen, being that tonight seemed to be a very unusual night, at least for me. My grandmother said that she was the crone witch and had her own part to play and that I could not pass this torch to anyone else. I had to say the blessing. This was because I was the eldest daughter, even if not by blood, of her eldest daughter. She was the eldest daughter of her mother Trisha Ellie, who was the eldest as well. I had to perform the ceremony as planned and practiced. I felt that I had no other choice. I was older, by quite a bit, than my sisters. Therefore, after all the tasks and preparations were complete, the ceremony began with a chant by my grandmother. I felt woozy, almost drunk, by the time that my turn came to say my blessing of the village. I felt like I was almost in a trance… Maybe I was. I was not feeling like myself, which was certain.

I started by asking the gods and Goddesses to bless the village and protect it from all harm. As I said my spell, there was a pale purple bubble forming around our village. All of the villagers were emotional to see this happen! I was still trancing a bit and did not really notice it at first. I was indeed floating by the time I was done asking for the protection of all that resided within our forest village! I felt as if I was shooting sparks from my fingertips and lightning from my Atheme! I was astounded to see so many people crying and laughing when I finished. Now that the ceremony had begun, the villagers sat with their personal alters in front of them and they began the to cast spells in unison to help with our fall and winter ground crops, winter hunting, and the births of healthy children. All spells were chanted in unison by every one of the villagers, while I was led away to my home, to rest by grandma rose…

಑

We reached my hut and she led me to the bed. I sat on the bed in front of my scrying bowl. I could only look at myself. I felt like I was a different person. I felt electrified! Moreover, I truly was, I was still glowing, and full of energy. Just *now,* I had no way to expel it. I decided that I would try to find a way to stop glowing first and think about it later. I picked up a crystal that my great grandmother had given me years ago when I was very small and tried the charging spell that I had been taught. I held the stone in my projective hand and visualized the light leaving me and entering the crystal. I asked Tara, the Goddess of peace and protection to grant me the power to release the light into the crystal. I held the crystal above my head and lowered it to my forehead. I finished with my spell and opened my eyes. I was no longer glowing. It had worked! My grandmother had been observing me while I preformed my spell. I felt as though I was transforming somehow into something or someone else.

Grandmother Rose asked me *"How did you know to do that?"* I said, *"It just came to me... I do not know how, it just did. Like a voice in my head, or an impression on my soul. I just knew!"* My grandmother went to the fire to brew me some passionflower tea to help me sleep. I went to bed and had a mostly uneventful night *except for the dream…*

ॐ

Late that night, I had a dream about people I did not think I knew, and it frightened me a little. It only frightened me to a point though. I was mostly bemused. I was seeing unknown people in places I have never been. It was actually a little nice to be able to travel in my mind's eye. I was seeing a large body of water. There were high cliffs and stone buildings. It was very dark outside; even the moon was not much help. These buildings looked like a place of worship and I liked them. There were not many trees, like what I have grown up with in the forest. I wonder, am I seeing the past or the future, or is this simply just a dream? Well, at the moment, I guess it does not really matter. I felt totally in control of the dream, and I looked around. I felt as though I was actually there. I saw the green, lush, healthy grass. It grew to the middle of my calf. I walked thru the grass, it was wet with dew, and I could feel its dampness. I came upon one of the stone buildings and approached it with care; I felt there was danger, though I could tell not what from. I had never seen structures made of stone and wood before. I walked along the side of the building dragging my hand upon the smooth, cool stone. It was so cool that it seemed to sweat, even in the cool air. I came to a doorway made of stone and oak. I read the door "O'Mear Inn". I could read the writing even though I had never seen the type of letters before. The letters were more like symbols than any letter I had ever seen. This is how the letters appeared to me, " ОэΜεαρ Iνν ". Yes, I know, I should not know how to read such writing, though I do, somehow I do. I slowly opened the heavy oak door and looked around. There was no light and I had to look for a candle. I reached into my waist purse looking for a matchstick and pulled out my glowing Chrystal. As I stood in the dark, I closed my eyes, I felt the warmth of the light flowing throughout my body and somehow I felt safer. I opened my eyes and noticed the whole room was lit up with the most brilliant light. I was glowing again! How am I able to turn it back on without thinking about it? I guess it was just a dream and all things are possible in dreams, or perhaps this is in the future somewhere else. I looked around the room I was standing in and it was mostly empty. There was a small table with two chairs, they were made of white oak, I do not recognize the artisanship, and I wonder who made it.... I turned and noticed that there was a long counter top that held a book. I walked over and looked at the book. It was written in the same strange writing as the door. It held a list of names and room numbers; it was a ledger book of the visitors to this inn. There was nothing else in this room. I noticed a set of stairs that was behind the entrance door. Across the room was another door. I walked over to it and when I reached for it, there was a bright flash of light and I heard a scream...an ear piercing, heart stopping scream...!

Then, I awoke with a start... I sat in my bed, in a mind haze, thinking about the dream for quite a while. Where was I?

Who was screaming? What was the

bright flash of light?

It took me quite a while. Although, When I finally lay back down, I fell asleep almost at once.

Chapter 4

"Transformations"

I awoke early the morning of November first and looked around. It was still dark outside. I knew that as soon as the day breaks, Cousin Tia and Grandma Rose, if I can still call them these sentiments, would be here to get me off on my journey. I felt different, like I was transforming, and although everything looked the same, I guess I could just tell something was off. I had the strangest feeling that today was just the first of many odd days to come.

As I retrieved my bedroll and gathered my supplies, I thought about what had happened the previous night. I found it difficult to believe what had happened to me in such a short amount of time. As I thought about myself glowing the way I did, I looked at my crystal, which is all it took to reaffirm that last night had really happened. The crystal was still glowing. I naturally was amazed! I reached out for it and placed it in my waist purse. I made sure to bring all of my personal belongings and my gold coins as well. I packed my personal travel alter and my Wiccan tools. I packed my only iron pot and some salted meat products. I can always get my vegetable items from the forest. I have always been a self-sufficient person and I know what is poisonous and what is not. My grandmother and mother taught me well. Although we usually grew our own vegetables and herbs, I sometimes ventured a short distance into the woods to gather mushrooms, berries, and naturally growing *herbs and vines.*

My leopard cub, King, would of course be taking this journey with me. I had only had him for a year, but I could not see myself leaving without him. He was a little wary of me this morning as though he felt something was different as well. I brought his bedding and food items. I guess that I am ready for my trip, although I am a bit scared to find out who and what I will find on my venture through the Foothill Forest and beyond.

I sat down in front of my scrying bowl once again and looked at my reflection. I looked different; I just could not tell what it was. My eyes are still emerald green, maybe just a little greener. My hair is still bright yellow blonde, maybe just a little lighter. I am still the same size, though I still feel that something is different about me. I just cannot put my finger on it...

ଔ

Grandma Rose and Tia arrived and brought Tia's horse and wagon to carry our belongings. I placed all of my items in the back under the cloth. I gave my grandma a warm hug goodbye and I promised that I would soon return. I know she was sad to see me leave, although somehow she looked at me differently in this morning's light. It was most unsettling. What is it that is different about me? Why have things changed about me so suddenly? I feel so heavyhearted to know that I am no longer the same as I was when I woke yesterday. Talk about growing up overnight!

Tia was not only my cousin, she has always been my best friend as well... We share all and repeat to none. The very best of friends! As much as I would like to have Tia on this journey with me, I just do not feel that it would be right to take her away from her duties in the village. I also do not wish for any harm to come of her. I feel this will be a most dangerous trip. If anything were to befall my best and dearest friend, I could live no longer! I will be sad to tell her that I cannot let her go past the creek with me on my trip...

As we started out, Tia was leading her horse and rigging. We were really speaking to each other a lot. Like girls sometimes do if they had not seen each other in a few moons. Tia wanted to know everything about last night. Like, what did glowing feel like, and did I feel different when I cast the circle, or did I know the purple bubble was forming, she was full of questions like that. We discussed it for quite a while. However it really did not matter how good the company and conversation was. I was mainly lost in thought. I am sure that is expected after such a shocking night full of power and revelations. Tia told me at one point that she had arranged for us to meet a hunter, a warrior, and a true forest guide near the creek, the very creek I was found at. I said that was a delightful idea to have such men in our party. Then we spoke about my crystal and the spell that helped me to stop glowing. Then not much was said after these words were spoken as we neared the forest thick, we were mainly looking out for animals and wild dogs, Forest people and such.

We arrived at the designated

meeting area only to find that no one was there…

Chapter 5

"The Journey Begins"

Tia was worried. I only figured that maybe we were early or they had not left on time. Tia said, "*No*, this is not possible. The men I have chosen are dependable men and would not just leave us in the forest alone. They must be here somewhere."

"It must be the wrong spot." I said, "And if what you tell me is true, then they must be either here or farther down the creek. We might have missed the mark and need to travel up or down stream a little or, they might be searching for food or following tracks." I said, "It's so hard to tell in the forest, the trees are so thick in areas, they could be only a short distance from here, and we would never see them for the trees."

Tia answered, "Yes, I know you are right. I just have a bad feeling. Maybe we should wait and leave in a day or two."

"*NO!*" I shouted at her. "You have never been told that you don't belong, you could never understand why it must be today. Really it should have been thirty years ago! I know it will be a dangerous trip, However, I also know I need to make it!"

"Now, Melinda, You did not mean that." Tia quietly replied, "You have always been happy in our village and you were well taken care of. Your parents were searched for. They were just never found. As you will soon see, this forest seems to go on forever. It is a hard forest to trek through." She paused and sighed, "I am just saying that with our party not arriving on time at this spot at the designated time, just, and maybe it's a bad omen."

I informed Tia, "Well then, if you are so worried maybe you should just turn around and go back to your village. I can continue alone if I must."

I wanted to cry, I could not believe that Tia would try to make me turn around. After all, it was *her* idea to leave today, to search at all, and that it be this morning! Now she just wanted to turn around and go home as if it did not matter. I guess that I *was* going to make her turn around and go back to the village, and leave out on my own, *anyway*. So why did it upset me so much that she doesn't want to go farther now? I *need* to make this trip! Our party has not arrived yet and I feel like I am in a hurry. Why do I feel like I am in a rush? What are a few more minutes or days, really? Why is it all of a sudden so urgent that we make this trip? Why has all of this started now? What was so special about my 33rd birthday that would change me so much in just a short while? What, with gaining these powers and finding out that I do not belong to the people I have always known as family, I almost felt let down. Abandoned, Lost, and scared, that is what I felt like! I know something is different about me, though I still have not figured it out yet. "Tia, I feel that I need to do this, Can you not understand? Why did you think I had to take this trip today? It was your idea in the first place." Tia only looked away from me and quietly apologized.

Now I was starting to get worried about

the men not arriving yet, too. So, to distract Tia and occupied myself, I decided that it was time for some wild herb tea and a nice fire, being that it was starting to get cool out. Tia gathered the twigs and moss to start a fire with while I gathered some fall berries and herbs for tea. Due to the chill in the air, and the long wait for the men to arrive, we also set up a shelter of sorts using the wagon and the old cloth on the back of it. As I drank my tea, sitting in our makeshift shelter, I brought out my crystal and looked at it. It was still glowing and it felt warm in my hand. I closed my eyes and let the warmth flow through my body. I started to feel better when I heard a noise coming from the woods behind the wagon. It did not sound like the footsteps of Three grown men, It did not really sound like footsteps at all, what was it? I slowly turned around and looked around the woods. I saw nothing, although I felt that someone was watching me. Tia was over by the creek, at the head of the horse, washing her face So, I decided that I would look around our campsite to find out what the noises were. As I started to turn around, I saw five men approaching our campsite, coming from the same direction of the village. Although I was alarmed at first, I alerted Tia that I thought that our party had arrived. Tia stood and immediately walked over to greet them. I stood starring into the forest in the opposite direction from where the men had come from. As the forest appeared before, it was still quiet. I went to the fire and started to put it out. Tia came over to me and said, "These men are the three we were awaiting and two of their comrades. Our venture will not be delayed any longer." Tia and I put out the fire, gathered our few belongings, and put them away, as the men loaded theirs. We re-rigged the horse to the wagon and King jumped into the back of the wagon as well. I might tell you, I would love to be riding up there myself, had the wagon been any bigger. As it was, a very small wagon was smaller than the horse that pulled it. It barley holds our things *and* King, my leopard. No one could ride the horse either due to the low hanging limbs of the oaks and ash trees. Therefore, we shall all walk, at least for now.

Chapter 6

"Introductions"

The five men were not altogether remarkable in looks; they were all rugged, and unkempt. Their names were Friedrich, Joseph, Keith, Kyle, and Thomas. I knew Thomas from the village as a hunter. However, I never before have seen the other four men. We started walking farther into the forest and I was glad for another woman's company after all, and so I never again told Tia to return home, and she did not leave me as I had told her too previously.

Tia and I followed behind the wagon watching that our belongings did not fall out.

We as well were watching King sleep. He is always sleeping during the day. I was a little afraid that he would leave and never return when it became dark out now that we are out in the forest. He is a natural hunter even though he has always been around people. I found him while I was on one of my ventures into the forest to collect something or another. King had a broken hind leg when i found him. He had been abandoned by his mother. I took him to the village where he was healed by my grandmother Rose. I tried to return him to his place in the forest, though he refused to stay. He followed me back home and has stayed with me over the last year. I miss him when he leaves me to hunt. I fear one day he will not return to me. I know he needs to be in the forest with his kind, although I would miss him terribly. Tia and I discussed what I was thinking about, and why I felt this was to be a dangerous trip. I assured her that not all of my creepy feelings meant something. I might just feel danger because I am nervous to find out where I am from.

Keith and Kyle, Who are twins, were farther behind us. They each had black hair and dark brown eyes. They seemed to be in their mid-forties and full of life. They were warriors and were on the constant watch for raiders and other people we did not know from the forest. You see, the forest is full of wild people who attack anyone they find in the forest. They will take anything they can and sometimes murder to get it. I am afraid to be this far from the shelter of our forest village. The wild people are not the only things we need to be wary of. There are also animals that would sooner kill you than look you in the eye as well.

We definitely need to keep a careful watch out. Our lives depend on it. Therefore, I am glad to see two warriors in our party as we trek through the rest of the forest.

Friedrich has brown hair and almost black eyes. He is about thirty and well built. He lives in the forest not really belonging to just one village; he travels a lot from land to land. We were lucky that he was available to us for this journey. He is a true forest guide. He was out in front; he will be leading us on our venture. I hear from Tia, that he can track anything and anyone. I just hope that he can lead us thru the forest even though neither he nor anyone else had ever been out of the forest that we know of. I am glad that he is here, nonetheless, even though I never met him before. He might not belong to any one village, though I do not believe him to be a dangerous wild forest person either.

Now, Joseph and Thomas are hunters and they will be watching for signs of animals to keep us fed. They were leading our horse and watching the forest. Joseph is thirty-eight and Thomas is forty-two. They each had red hair and blue eyes. Of course, it was nice to have two hunters in the party. Therefore, if one does not hunt well, then at least the other one might catch enough to feed us that night. At least that is the way it would seem to me. Tia said that it was just as easy for both of the hunters to not locate any prey as it was for one of them to fail. I never really look at things the same way that Tia does. I feel that two hunters mean that we now have twice the chances of eating, than if only one of them had come with our party.

I feel highly privileged to have five men to protect Tia and me, although I am sure Tia can hold her own against any of the roughest toughest men you could throw at her. As far as i go, well, I would not be so lucky. I would probably faint at the sight of any man charging at me with the thought of malice on his mind! I am not afraid to admit that I am a weakling. I have never before been able to stomach a good fight.

We had been walking for hours when we decided to stop and rest the horse. We all ate a little and talked less. The guide was looking around the forest at the edge of our makeshift supper camp for tracks and trails. The hunters were working on traps and rope. Moreover, our warriors were keeping a low profile watch while they snacked on dried deer flank. Tia and I were busy feeding ourselves, King, and of course the horse. We were all so busy that we really were not having many conversations. We all finished our chosen chores. We put our things back on the wagon. Then it was forward on the trail again.

I walked with Tia for another four hours, discussing all we were seeing, and what we thought we might find out about my own village or people. I mentioned that I would defiantly like to join up with our guide, if he will have me to teach. I know every animal that lives in this forest. I am sure he could teach me quite a bit about tracking them. I felt that this was a great idea. Therefore, we discussed it seriously.

Tia said, "If this is what you want

to do, it is completely up to you. I will not be far from you should you need anything. If you should decide that you do not want to develop a tracker sense then all you have to do is excuse yourself and return to my side. I would be glad to have you walk beside me" Hearing this made me feel great about wanting to learn and I walked ahead to meet up with our tracker, Friedrich. I was excited and hoped he would not mind teaching me as we made our trip into the unknown. It was almost time to make camp, so I felt that this was a good time to discuss with him my thoughts.

Chapter 7

"A Blood Curdling Scream"

As I reached the front where Friedrich was, I had not gotten the chance to ask him of his teachings, when there was a woman's scream from deep in the forest, somewhere ahead! Friedrich and I stopped in mid stride and hurriedly took cover behind a group of white oak trees. Our Warriors, Keith and Kyle, ran past us. They had run so far ahead that we could no longer see them. There was an eerie silence following the scream. Tia ran up and joined us behind the trees. Tia was white as a ghost! I could tell she was frightened, I wondered if I looked just as scared and she did. The hunters of our party, Joseph and Thomas, separated and watched us from a distance on each side, also keeping watch to the front and rear. I heard another scream and I thought that I recognized it as the same scream from my dream. No, it could not be. Who would I know that would be this far out into the forest? I was beginning to worry that my dream was a dream of the future, a precognitive dream that only seers' have. I was thinking about my dream, and whether or not to tell Tia, when suddenly Tia grabbed my shoulder, She Scared heavens out of me! I looked at her and her face was oddly contorted, I looked in the direction that she was staring. What I saw was unbelievable!

There was a man dressed in a

copper red shirt and brown leather pants. He was Levitating above a large, fallen tree, which was lavishly adorned in green Irish moss. He was about four foot six inches tall. He has blond hair, like me! He had his arms raised to the sky and was chanting in a low voice. We could not make out what he was saying, though we all knew it was a spell of sorts.

I felt as though I knew him, but how could I. I was only three when I was found, and I have never since been out of the general area of the village or the closely surrounding forest. We were walking all day thru this forest and it was about time to set camp when we heard the screams. Therefore, I knew it was about to be dark. I had to see what the unknown man was doing. I had to see his eyes! I feel a connection to this man I just cannot explain it! I know he resembles me, but he cannot be much younger than me. Could he be my brother? If he is my brother, why was he not left with me when i was three? Maybe he is another relative, either way it would be nice to speak to him… However, I am so frightened. I cannot seem to talk myself into moving. I feel so mesmerized by just watching what he is doing. He is chanting a spell, I am sure of it. What is the spell for, I wondered. All of us only sat and watched him it was a spectacular sight. I need to see his eyes! I cannot help but feel that seeing his eyes would set the world spinning. If I could only get over there, close enough to him to see his EYES, I would be splendidly ecstatic!

I heard another scream and realized that this man was floating over a woman with a flowing red renaissance gown and fire red hair. I did not feel that he was trying to hurt her; however, I did feel that she was in danger! How could I be getting such mixed signals? I felt like my head was spinning! Her screams were so loud and completely desperate. Now it seemed as though it took every ounce of my internal force and energy to not run to this young, very young woman's aide.

৪৩

Tia was so still that I had almost forgotten that she was there until I heard her rapidly breathing into my ear. She was scared stiff and it was I that wanted to rush to this woman's' side. Quite the opposite for us both, as it would seem now, neither one of us were acting ourselves at all. I was willing to go, however I knew that our warriors were out there and might hit one of us with their arrow if we ran out now, so we must stay still for the moment. I asked Tia in a hushed voice if she needed to lie down… She said she did not feel well and would like to get into the wagon with king until this was over. I had Friedrich help her quietly to the wagon.

I continued to watch the man and young woman. I felt that if I could hear what was being chanted that I could better assess the situation. I needed a way to find out if he was friend or foe, as well as what he was doing with this woman in the middle of the forest. It was beginning to get dark; I worried about where the worriers were. They had seemed to run well into the forest ahead of us. This means that with dark upon us, they might not be able to come back until first light. We were on or own in the woods, with this odd spectacle happening in front of us. I motioned for the hunters to rejoin me at the trees. They did, and we tried to figure out what we would do next. As it would seem to all involved, that we were going to have to camp without a fire, we unhitched the horse and tied her off. We left Tia in the wagon; she seemed to have broken into fever and would need some feverfew by morning to snap her out of this condition that has befallen her. We huddled at our spot beneath the oaks and tried to keep warm while watching this stranger casting spells over the woman before him on the large fallen tree. I chose to keep watch first. I wanted to ease a little closer to the fallen tree so that I could hear what he was saying. I am just guessing here, however I feel that he has been at the chants for a long few hours. I looked into my waist purse and saw my crystal was still glowing. I took it out and tied it to the top of my walking stick. I felt that I could get closer to him if I stayed directly behind him; this way he would never see me coming. With all the chanting from him and the now, quiet screams and squeals from the woman, I did not figure that he would hear me coming. I got very close to him and stood behind another large tree, which was enough to shield me from his sight if he were to turn around. I placed the crystal back into my waist purse and peeked out to see what could be seen. I was unable to tell from my earlier distance; however, I now noticed that he was glowing with a faint yellow light. The woman was also glowing only her light was a dull red color. I was astounded to see this! That is one of my powers! We must be family! We must be! I made a sudden and frightening decision to try to make myself glow without lighting a torch. I took out my crystal and just reversed what I had done to stop glowing. I held the crystal above my head and envisioned the light returning to me and leaving the Crystal…IT WORKED!

I cannot believe that I had made it work! My power seems to be growing. I could no longer sense the two people before me. I felt a little light headed. I can see that they went nowhere, although they seemed to have disappeared. It only happened when I started glowing again. Maybe it is like if you lose one sense, you gain another. This is the sort of thing that happens only to the elder people in Hill Dale. It feels so different to not sense what you can see right in front of you, Unusually odd if you ask me.

Chapter 8

"Curiosity"

I had been standing in the forest watching this man chanting for a while now. As dark as it was out, my exquisite glows being white in color, and so bright, that I lit up the entire surrounding area. This included where we were camped and where the man stood over the woman. The blond haired man was chanting a spell until I started glowing. He turned to look at me. I was no longer frightened. What I saw in his eyes was sadness and compassion, though I could not tell the color from our distance. I could tell that he loved this woman; I could see it in his eyes. I started to walk over to them and realized that I was not walking but rather gliding a few inches off the ground. I am now levitating too! Wow, it just never ends. I said a small quiet spell of protection for this woman under my breath and a light purple glowing bubble formed around her. The blond man slowly stepped down from the fallen tree. He held his hands out to me. I was still gliding toward him. I felt as though he was frightened of me and was scared of what I might do. The woman let out a shrill scream that was far louder than any she had released thus far. I could tell that my bubble of protection was helping her to regain her strength. As I reached the man and stood in front of him, he dropped to one knee, and asked for my forgiveness. He called me Goddess. Why would he call me Goddess? I spoke only to tell him that none was needed and that he should stand and go to his loves side. I fear that he mistakes me for someone or something other than myself. He did as he was told, though he watched me. I asked, "What is your name, my gentleman? "

He slowly replied, "My name is Morgan, My family is not from here. Please forgive me Goddess, for trespassing into this magical forest, Please, I mean no harm!"" I asked him his loves name. "My lady, her name is Meagan, My dear sister. She is ill, and I am here in this magical place to ask the goddess' and gods' to relieve her of her pain and sickness. Will you help us; she needs your protection and blessing if she is to survive this illness."

"Morgan, I must ask… May I see your eyes?" I quietly requested. "Why, yes, my lady…. I will let you see my eyes. My only request is that you help my sister to be well again. Surely any great Goddess as your self can manage this with no great effort." I answered, "My dear Morgan, I am not a great Goddess of any kind." He replied "Then you are the greatest of all Sorceresses that I have ever seen or heard of"

I answered his plea with" Morgan, I am new to my powers and have yet to practice or explore them. I will help you in any way that I might. Rest assured that I would help your sister to regain some strength and energy. I will do my best, but I must see your eyes, please I must."

Morgan stood and walked up to me; I looked into his eyes and knew at once that he was family. "Morgan? I must now ask you to reveal your full-imparted name. What is your family name, Please, I must know it." Morgan looked a little upset at this request,

"Miss, why do you need my family name? It cannot possibly help in any way to heal my sister. Please, must I tell you? Cannot you just help my sister; she hasn't much time left I fear!"

I felt bad for asking such a question that makes him so nervous, before trying to help him. I agreed to help him. I went to Meagan's side. I reached through the pale purple bubble and I placed my projective hand onto her forehead and my receptive hand onto her lower abdomen, I asked the Goddess Brighid for the return of this Young woman, Meagan's, energy and wellbeing. As said my spell and envisioned this young woman returning to her feet, she screamed again! SO LOUD! SO LOUD! I almost faltered; I tried again, and again. When I opened my eyes, the purple bubble surrounded Meagan and me with such a light that I could not see the forest. I looked down at Meagan and saw that she was looking at me. I risked talking. "How are you feeling my lady?" She looked at me for a few, then she answered, "Yes, I feel better… The pain has gone. I am no longer with fever. I wonder how this can be. Where is my brother Morgan? Please, tell me of his safety…..Please. I have to know that he is safe." I assured her of his safety and told her to rest so she may get well. We sat for a while together in my bubble. I asked her to tell me what it is like where she is from. She turned her head and tears flowed freely. "Miss, I fear to tell you that our land has been overrun with the outsiders and they have stolen most our children. They have spent thirty-five years collecting our children and we never see them again. My brother and I were hiding in a forgotten area of our land when

I fell ill. Our land used to be a magical place of paradise, The Fae used to reside there as well. We have great waterfalls and lakes and streams, the plant life is like none I've seen elsewhere." This is when Meagan fell asleep once more; I asked no more from dear Meagan, at this time. I simply let her rest. I chanted a low, however, constant spell of healing and protection for Meagan.

Chapter 9

"A Healing Spell"

As we sat in the purple bubble regaining strength and much needed energy, I looked into Meagan's eyes when she opened them again. She had the same green eyes as me and Morgan, though she had red hair rather than blond. We shared facial features that I was sure she was taking note of as well as I. As she healed, Meagan began to move around. I asked her what her sickness was. "I'm not sure at all. My brother and I had been in a remote location hidden near our cottage. I fell ill and Morgan was told to bring me here, to these woods. His spells were not strong enough to save me. I felt like I would never survive. I then awoke in here with you. What is your name my lady?"

I answered cryptically, "My name is Melinda. That is all you need to know at this time. We will have more time to speak when you are fully well again. No more talking, just for now. Try to rest Meagan."

As I held her, I looked at her features and saw my eyes and my mouth. Although she has fire red hair, she has my chin. I could not help but to notice that she was the same size as me as well. I have never seen in the faces of all my loved ones anything that remotely resembled me. It saddens me to realize that I truly did not belong in Hill Dale after all. As I have stated before, I always knew I was different, now I truly understand. I was brought to tears. What if we were not really related, do they know my Fairling family? Will I learn the truth from these kind hearted people? Will my trip have to continue farther?

Morgan stood outside the bubble quietly watching, he could not see Meagan or Melinda anymore. Friedrich, Joseph, and Thomas were outside the bubble now as well. The bubble was pulsating different shades of purple. Friedrich asked Morgan a few quite questions and got no real answers. They all were worried but not overly concerned. It was almost daybreak so, the hunters decided to try and find some quail eggs and a small hog for breakfast. They set out on the hunt. Keith and Kyle, the worriers, wondered up on the bubble and asked Friedrich what was going on. "We were all sleeping and Melinda was standing first watch. We awoke to another scream and we noticed that Melinda was not in our camp. We saw a white glowing figure and heard some more chanting, it seems that Melinda is healing this man's sister. She fell ill sometime back and he was told to bring her here to cast some healing spell. It was not working so Morgan here says Melinda said a spell and this purple bubble appeared. We ran over here to find out what was happening. Melinda and Meagan have been in there for several hours now, all night as it is. I am beginning to worry." Friedrich answered.

Keith said, "During our All hallows Eve ceremony a similar bubble appeared surrounding the entire village. It stayed in place until the sun rose. No one could come in or out before it disappeared. So, possibly this bubble will dissipate at sunrise too. All we can do is wait it out. It might not disappear until Meagan is well again. So we must go to our chores and allow it to stay its course." Keith was not worried about Melinda or Morgan's' Sister Meagan. He felt that we would all know soon enough what would come next. Keith and Kyle watched the forest to protect Melinda if anything else were to occur.

Morgan was tired. He went to the camp and lay down on a bedroll to try to sleep. Friedrich walked the horse to an area to graze, while he tried to locate some water in the still dark morning. It is all he could do until daybreaks.

Joseph and Thomas came back to the camp and started a fire to cook their catch. Tia was still with fever in the wagon, so they all let her sleep.

Melinda and Meagan were still safe within their

bubble of purple. Everyone tried to busy themselves to

make the camp ready for the two women when the

emerged from the bubble.

Chapter 10

"QUESTIONS ASKED"

As the sun rose and the sunlight hit the bubble, it slowly became dimmer until it was completely gone. Meagan and I both stood and walked slowly to the camp area. Neither one of us were glowing now. I was drained, completely. I felt more tired than I had ever been before in my whole life. Meagan was not sick anymore, though, she needed quite a bit of rest still. When we arrived over at the campsite, the food was done and smelled wonderful! Neither one of us were going to sleep until we received food. Though questions were asked of us, we both waved them off politely and explained that we needed to rest before we could answer any questions. I quietly checked on my friend Tia, who was feeling better after having breakfast, though she remained in the wagon. She too needed much rest, we were unsure of why she had developed a fever, so we kept her as comfortable as we could in the wagon for now. Tia somehow thought that she fell ill when we wondered upon Meagan while she was ill. Now that Meagan was better, so was Tia. I wonder if Tia were partly an empathic, how else would she feel Meagan's sickness. Had she somehow developed the same sickness that Meagan had had? If so, why had she found herself better only after I had healed Meagan. It is all so confusing…

I still know so little about my powers, even though I do know a lot about magical powers in general. I know that glowing and levitating was never on the list when I was being taught about magical powers. Neither were any of the protection bubbles nor the shimmering circles. This was all new to me. I still cannot imagine what all my powers are. I know that I am a healer, all I have to do is think about things and I can make them happen so far. Maybe I am really a sorceress; I cannot explain it any other way. I am thrilled but also scared, what other magic can I do? I will just have to find my own people to have these questions answered.

We women ate and then lay down next to the fire to sleep until we had regained our strength and energy. As we slept, our party hunters found more meat for dinner. We were to have pork again. It is a great meat when caught wild, I am sure that we can all agree on this as a whole. Friedrich scoped out the area for tracks and trails, found a nicely worn trail that led him to a deep creek, it was almost a river it was so wide. Our warriors, Keith and Kyle, sharpened their tools and helped Friedrich out when he went to the creek. Joseph and Thomas set the fire and gathered water, cooked our dinner and made a nice herb salad. We were to be well fed tonight. I believe if they had all the makings, that they would have made bread or pie! Meagan had a hard time sleeping and was awake most of the day, although she stayed in her borrowed bedroll until dinner was prepared. . I was the opposite; I slept hard as a rock. I do not believe I have ever slept as well as I did that day. The smell of food only barley awakened my senses.

       At about time to reset camp, I arose and Friedrich said we were moving the camp. I wondered why, though I was still too tired to ask about the why is just yet. We rigged the horse, located King, and all moved our things to the creek. I noticed that there was a small area that made a kind of pond. I also noticed that there was a waterfall up creek from us. It all was so lovely. I was glad for the clean water and decided to get in after we were all settled. I felt that the water, even with as cool as I knew it was going to be, would help me to finish my recuperation. I suggested that Meagan and Morgan get in, as well as the other five men. I thought it would do us all good. Most agreed and joined me, though Thomas was worried that the food would get cold or overcooked if he did not watch it. Therefore, he stayed out. You would have thought that being the beginning of November and the air being slightly frigid that none of us would find ourselves sitting in a small cold pond discussing the day that had just left us. However, that is just where we found ourselves.

As we all sat in the cool water, it began to shimmer around Meagan. I noticed it, though no one else seemed to. It was a blue tinted light that surrounded only Meagan and I knew it had to mean something. We sat in the cool water discussing the night before and what all I had accomplished as well as the day that we missed while we slept. Everyone seemed greatly amazed, except for Meagan and Morgan, though no one was as amazed as I was. I was distracted by the blue shimmering light that surrounded Meagan and could not contain it any longer. I asked, "Meagan, do you know that the water is dancing around you like blue flames?" Meagan replied, "Yes, I am aware of it, though I did not know anyone could see it except for me. How do you perceive it? I mean, what do you see exactly?" I told her, "It looks like light blue shimmering light. It is faint, though I can see it. Why is the water lit up around you and none other?" Meagan said, "I am related to a great sorceress named Morrigan. She was Morgan's and my grandmother. She was a very powerful Wiccan sorceress. Although, I take after my mother, Maya. She was not as powerful as Morrigan; however, it still runs in our veins to be as powerful. One woman from every generation is as great, or greater, a sorceress and Morrigan was. I am with child. My daughter will be a great sorceress, though I am sure not as great as our grandmother was. In addition, if you notice all of our family has names beginning with "M", it is not a coincidence. The "M" names help to empower us and protect us. It is said that over 500 years ago, there was a curse placed on our family by a neighboring village, which prevents us from wielding our goddess given Wiccan powers. This curse was cast by another family from our island from another village. They believed that no one except for them should have the right to have and use magic. We overcame this curse when finally after 300 years or more, we found out all of us with an "M" name was spared from this curse. We found out a way to regain and use our powers and have named our children accordingly. You may also have noticed that the women of our clan have names of goddess', this is believed to help us to commune with our deities' better, to make us stronger yet."

Morgan and the other men only sat and listened while Meagan spoke to me. I was sure that they were just as interested as I to learn where these folks were from.

I asked, "Meagan, your brother said if I could help you to regain your health and I helped to spare your life, he would indulge me with your family name, Pray-tell, whatever is it? If it isn't so rude of me to ask, I hope that it would be alright to let me know." Meagan interrupted me, and said, "Melinda, do not despair so. I will tell you what you need to know, you have saved my life. I am an open book, only for your reading pleasure." I replied, "You see, I am looking for a family and I feel that you can help me. I have only just started to gain my powers, on All Hallows

Eve, and am in desperate need to find my roots."
Meagan said " If you need our family name I will be
all too happy to divulge it to you, Our families
imparted name is "Fairling", May I ask the family you
seek?"

I could not answer, because I passed out.
I was carried from the creek and dried. I was laid to
rest by the fire, with King at my side all night.

Chapter 11

"A Special Meeting"

I dreamed again that night... It was an odd dream to say the least.   I was looking over a large body of water; I could not see land across it. I had a feeling that I was surrounded by water. Morgan, Meagan, and Tia were there beside me. Tia looked lost and confused. I could not read the faces of Meagan or Morgan at this time. I felt Tia's presence, though I could not sense Meagan or Morgan. I felt a little like I was seeing into a tunnel. All the edges of the dream were almost blurred. Meagan was indeed with child although she was now far along and showing. I could tell her child was to be a girl and she was strong and healthy. She was to be called Marinna. I do not doubt this, and I know this is a dream of the future, even while I am having it. I know; it is a little odd. It is new to me too.

I turned around and looked at my surroundings. We were in a village, small though it is. There were people busy with chores designated by their status in the village. There were a few women watching over the children while others carried water, tanned animal skins, prepared meals, or cleaned huts. There did not seem to be many men in the village, the sun was high in the sky, they must be hunting or checking traps. The men that were there shooed small children away as they sat, smoking, and talking together. Yet others were building or repairing homes and other structures. I felt as though I was seeing this village after an awful storm. As I looked around farther I saw there was debris and damages in the northern part of the village, and the southernmost part of the village seemed in better shape. I walked away from the water and to the east. I saw a forest and a few stone structures. I knew one of these from my first dream. It was the Inn. I did not need to enter there, so I walked past it still heading east. I seemed to have traveled hours in just minutes. I saw that I was coming to another body of water. There were fishermen and some small huts. I saw a few carved out trees that were floating on the water. Meagan told me "Those are boats," as she pointed to the floating trees. I did not know this word, boats. However, I did not question her about it. It seemed that this village was full of life, even as it smelled like death. All the people I saw were happy and healthy, I could not read, or sense them either. I found this strange. I never, before now, realized that I could sense people so well, or the way they were feeling. I now feel oddly empty. The only person I could feel was Tia. I know where she is, what she is feeling, and that she is scared. I know I am on Meagan and Morgan's Island, as she called it. I am guessing that they have blocked their feelings and thoughts from other people so that they can live here without other people finding them. I turned and started back to the west and found the sun was setting. I could not see water in the west, so I had a long walk. I lit a few torches and started glowing. I led Meagan, Morgan, and Tia back to the west. We came to a large enclosed hut made of cut trees and stone. There was an indoor fire. I worried the place was burning. As

Meagan took the lead and knocked on the wooden door, I looked around the hut. There was an herb and vegetable garden. There were goats and cages with weird looking birds in them.

A mid aged woman with, ankle length, blond hair opened the door. Her ears were pointed like the Elvin people I once met from the Foothill Forest. She wore a long white house gown, with a stitched on pattern, with a white cloak, which was made of a soft fuzzy cloth, and her feet were bare. Her eyes were green; I knew this was my mother. She was strikingly beautiful. We looked alike, even as I was younger. I felt my ears and noticed they were too were pointed like this woman's were. THAT IS what was different the morning our trip started. As I looked in the scrying bowl, I had seen though not really noticed MY EARS! Meagan and Morgan's ears were also pointed. Why had I not noticed it before? My eyes were a little more slanted and my chin a little more pointed now as well. Am I transforming into Elvin? It seems so. Just look at her, she looked so good! Wait! Why had she left me all those years ago and nowhere near this island? I opened my mouth to speak and I heard King growling. I felt like I was being pulled up thru layers of myself to come awake.

Chapter 12

"A Life Denied"

I lay very still and listened carefully. I heard King-growling low in his throat. I heard someone walking around in our camp; I could not tell who it was. The fire had died low, so I risked peeking out from under my lids. I saw Thomas, Friedrich, Keith and Kyle. They were loading up the wagon with their things and quietly placing our things aside on the ground. I did not know what to do. If I wake the rest of the party then a fight might ensue and deaths may occur. I kept quiet and let them leave, with our horse and wagon. I let them leave because they did not steal anything but the horse and wagon and I was afraid for our lives. They, after all, had left all of our other things for us. When they were out of the camp and I could no longer see the torches they carried, I sat up and let King know it was ok. I woke Tia, Meagan, and Morgan. Tia was furious! I knew she would be, though I reminded her that they did leave us our other belongings. She did not seem to care that they took her horse! "How could they steal our horse?" she said, "Why would they just leave us here?"

I asked, "Tia, why is the horse so important to you? We were going to have to leave her behind in our trek thru the woods, at some other point anyhow."

Tia said, "They took our gold and alter supplies Melinda! It was all in the horses saddle bags!"

"Oh, I see, well, we can make more alter supplies here in the woods and gold, well there wasn't much of that anyway." I said. "Meagan and Morgan are here with us as well as Joseph. We have a hunter with us, and Morgan came here, so maybe he knows the way out. We shall be fine... I have *seen* us on Meagan and Morgan's island. I have *seen* Meagan full with child; I know we shall be fine."

Morgan walked up to the fire where we ladies stood and informed all, "Joseph is dead. It looks like he was asleep when his throat was slashed; all of his things are gone. I am doubtful that he felt a thing. We shall bury him and say a spell to send him on his great journey through the heavens." I could only think how I am delightfully happy that I did not show that I was awake before the other men left. We sat at the fire and talked for a while.

"Melinda, Tia told us while you slept about our family names being the same. I know you are looking for your mother and father. "Morgan said.

Meagan continued, "We believe you to be our sister long ago lost. We were never told her name; however, she was three when she disappeared. Her birth date was October the 30th. If this is true, and you are her, then your mother is well. However, your father left to search for you and never returned. I am but twenty-five and Morgan is twenty-seven. We have a different father than you, if you are her, but we are still hopeful that you are our family."

"I was not surprised to hear you say the family name of Fairling. I noticed your features as my own while I looked into your face." I continued, "I was thrilled to hear you say this. Just for argument sake, I have already dreamed of my mother. She was beautiful. She has Elvin ears, like you and Morgan do. She was dressed in all white with bare feet. Her cloak was made of some kind of fuzzy soft cloth. Not quite a fur, but most like it. I have odd dreams and see places and people I have never before met. I think that my dreams are a little precognitive. I feel like I am there when I am dreaming. Tonight when I awoke to the men leaving with our things, I had awakened form a dream where I visited our mother. If I tell you that I know things, would that be too far from the truth you know?"

Morgan answered, "Not at all, we have precognitive dreams and visions as well. We can also sense things in people that they did not know or wish others to know. Other than our own people, we have a natural block that prevents anyone from knowing we are there, unless they physically see us."

"I am glad to know these things, for sure. What magical abilities do your people have?" I asked.

Meagan told me, "We have a variety of magic in our village; however none like yours, since grandmother died. You said that you came into your powers only all hallows eve?"

I said, "Yes, I celebrate this as my date of being born. I believe myself to be thirty-three. When do your villagers tend to develop their powers?"

Morgan said, "We usually have them

from birth and have to work hard to develop them as to not lose them. If you aren't taught how to use your certain powers you lose them and hardly ever regain them."

"Well, I had powers when I was about three, then I was taught healing spells. I was very good until I was ten or so, then I just could not wield magic very well. The night of all hallows eve, there was a full moon and all these things started to occur." I said. Then I divulged all that had happened the night of my birthday, all hallows Eve.

"That's not normal as far as I know; usually you retain some kind of power. You never completely loose them." Meagan said. "Though, none of our powers are as strong as yours, Except for the one female from every generation. We have never seen the protection bubble as you cast or heard of the shimmering circle developing before now."

Tia was first to say how tired she was, and all agreed that we would just wait until we reached the island before we get our hopes too high, though I knew we were all excited and hopeful even now! We finished resting up and we gathered our things and hiked through the woods for the rest of the night. We rested often and took turns keeping watch while we were stopped. We hunted small game and harvested herbs and wild vegetables to eat. We walked for fourteen days before we saw another person in these woods.

Chapter 13

"Cheese, Please"

We ventured onward, towards Meagan and Morgan's island. We only saw one other person on our journey thus far. She was an elderly woman with a herd of twenty "fainting" goats. She made cheese with their milk. Then she went to all the forest villages to trade it for things that she would need to keep herself through the year. Her name was Jessica. She welcomed us into her home and fed us. We were an extremely exhausted and hungry group.

It seemed like a lifetime since we had eaten cheese or drank milk. It was a nice treat to be sure, even though it had only been a moon or so since I had started this journey. We stayed with Jessica for two moons. We helped her to make her cheese; this was a learning experience for us all. We took to keep her heard fed. We cleaned her home and harvested herbs. We helped Jessica learn to dry them.

We said that on our way back to Hill Dale we would return and help her to the village to trade her cheese. I traded with Jessica my walking stick for some cheese to carry with us when we left. She needed the walking stick more than I did anyhow, As well as the cheese being a great food item to carry with us.

Meagan was now five moons along with child and she was starting to show. Morgan was anxious to go home to his wife, who is also with child, should be six or seven moons by now, Morgan figures. Her name is Morganna, She will be having a girl as well, we hope. Tia was having a hoot of a time being away from Hill dale. She believed that she might meet a gentleman on this trek and marry as well. I was not too hopeful to find someone and settle down. I was not really interested in marriage; I have yet to find a love yet as well. I know it is a part of life to reproduce. I am just not interested, at least not yet. I am too busy in the village for a husband or children anyway. I used to want them, but not so much anymore. Not since, I moved out on my own and know what it is like not to have to care for a house full. I feel so selfish at times, but that is ok for now.

We ventured on, traveling all day and resting at night. A moon later, we came to a large field with no trees. Morgan said, "We pass this land and we will be at the ocean. When we arrive there, there is a village that we can rest in. After we are well rested, we shall take a boat to our island. We will have to be careful and watch where we walk. There are animals here that you have never before seen. None is too dangerous alone, but if they group then we might have trouble. Meagan, you tell me if you need rest. We will have to find shade if we are to rest for any length of time, the sun will beat the breath from us if we aren't careful."

"Morgan, do we need to hunt or harvest herbs for the trip across this land? Or are there plants and animals to hunt once we get into this land?" I asked. "What is an ocean? I have never heard this word." I was a little worried and felt out of my element.

Morgan said, "There are no worries of food. We shall be fed. I will be sure of that. An ocean is the largest body of water seen by my people. We travel it by boat. There are many other lands we have found, none as magical as our own. Even the land we are on is surrounded by ocean. This Ireland is just one of many islands in this ocean. Ours is smaller though."

We made camp and waited for night to approach. Morgan caught a few rabbits and I made an herb salad. We ate well tonight for sure. I hope that things go well once we leave the forest edge. I will be glad to visit the island that I have dreamt of nightly since I passed out at the creek.

Chapter 14

"Elemental Boundaries"

We slept the night, before our journey was to continue through the grassland, where the forest ended and the land began. I was most thrilled and frightened at the same time. I had never before been out of the great Foot Hill forest. I was quite excited to be going to Meagan and Morgan's Island. I have only dreamt of the island, and though I feel I know every square inch of it, I would love to see it. I had a hard time sleeping that night, for the mixed feelings I was having. Meagan seemed to be uncomfortable on the ground tonight, I think she might be feeling the baby quickening. Tia and Morgan slept as though they had to out run a forest leopard today, like they were worn out or had no cares in the world. I kept the fire high and checked our supplies repeatedly. King my leopard cub was out on the prowl, I think he loves this grassland! I thought of the dreams that I have had nightly of this island, and I am sure we will make it there in good health. However, I feel it will take us some time to get there. When I finally did fall asleep, I was awaked by strange noises; I have heard them before, but when? Yes, I know. In the forest on our first day of this trip, I was going to investigate the noises when our party had arrived. I was suddenly frightened that the men who left our party and murdered Joseph had come back to rob or murder us, moons later, in our sleep. I did not rest the rest of the night. At sunrise, Morgan went out to catch rabbits and we ladies were left alone. I shared my night with Meagan and Tia. When I told of the noises, Meagan asked, "How do the noises sound?"

I answered, "It sounds like footsteps, or rather more like, like really fast wings moving dead leaves in the trees. I really cannot describe the noises; I have never known anything that makes these kinds of noises before."

Tia was on the edge of her fallen log with excitement and fright. Meagan continued, "You might be hearing Fae folk, did you consider this?"

I could only answer, "No, I have never seen or heard Fae folk before, I would not know what they sound like. Could it be? Have you ever seen or heard Fae folk before?"

Meagan said, "Why yes, we are distant cousins of the Fae folk and we transform into a larger variation of them as we age. You say it sounds like very fast wings as well as footsteps. It could be that a Fae was flying by or one of our people was in the area. There is also the possibility that it was a green forest dragon. They aren't very large, have you ever seen one of these?"

I shook my head "No", as Tia said, "I have never seen one, though I have heard of them before. They are not dangerous either. It could be that is all it was. I mean, really, Fae Folk, out here. It is not heard of in hill dale that a Fae would come away from home all alone. If you hear one of them you hear many, they never go along away from home, or so I hear."

Meagan replied, "This is not true. They have been known to explore alone, sometimes for moons at a time. Though to hear it more than once, maybe we have one following us."

ॐ

Morgan came back into our camp and asked us to ready ourselves to have our meal and then we would be leaving. We ladies packed while Morgan prepared our meal. Meagan discussed our talk with him; he felt it to be a green forest dragon. "They find humans curious so they like to follow and watch us. The green forest dragons are large enough to ride on, if you can find a way to train one. Although, they are clumsy little fellows. If you stay up alone outside in the night, they like to play; usually they pick one person to link to. You heard it the first time in the morning so, it might not be a dragon. However, it could have been the Fae, they too like to keep watch over humans they find worthy, and they too find us a curious bunch. We are related to the Fae, far removed mind you. That is how we have glowing abilities. A few of our distant ancestors mated with the Fae. The Fae are just smaller humans with wings, they have elfish features as well. That is why we have pointed ears and why we are smaller than the average human. As we age, we generally start to transform into larger Fae folk. Some things that may happen are, our ears get pointed, we sometimes grow wings, as well as losing our height sometimes. We can also cast some of the same magic as the Fae. Our peoples' size ranges from four to five foot, the Fae are in the two to three foot range, and humans grow to be five to six feet or better", Morgan said.

We ate our meal and started across the grassy land. We walked until the sun was too high in the sky to keep going. We found a tree to sit under and rest. Meagan was thankful for the rest, as well as getting out of the direct sunlight. Tia wandered around close by. She loved to look at everything and every animal we passed. She is a very curios person. However, she never slowed us down. However, she did have to catch up at times. We planned out our journey through the grassland. We would be resting and napping when the sun was high and we would be walking some after the sun set. We would make camp when we could not go farther.

Chapter 15

"THE STORM"

We followed this reasoning for the better part of a moon, and then a great storm came through. We had no shelter and had to huddle together to keep from being blown apart. Meagan was now full with child at seven moons and could not keep going like this, I asked Morgan while the storm was raging over us, "How many more days or moons till we reach your village of rest?"

He replied, "We should have been there already, if we did not need to rest so often we would have been there ten days ago or so. We should be there in a few days, with any hope, not much longer."

We ladies were glad to hear this and vowed we would try to walk more during the night to get there sooner. The storm had raged for many days already. We had to try to travel during it so we could, at the very least, find shelter for Meagan. She was not doing well, she was tired and sun burnt. We all were, only the sun had drained her more due to her being with child. We were now wet and chilled by the constant beating rain. The wind was worse than the sun; getting windburn is defiantly worse. The wind tears at your skin and causes water blisters faster than sunburn will blister you it seemed. We have to find shelter For Meagan if not for us all.

We traveled very slowly through the storm. We found a group of trees to help shelter Meagan and the rest of us. They were toppled from the storm, though they did provide some much-needed protection from the wind. We were soaked to the bone from the rain.

We were in the group of trees for three more days until the wind slacked and we were able to travel farther. We were hungry and tired. We were scared that the animals of this land were hungry, too. If they tracked us, we were moving so slowly that, they could get us to be sure. We kept a close eye out, and saw nothing. King was on high alert as well. King hunted small game and actually brought us some too. We could not braze the meat due to all the wood and grass being wet, so we ate it raw, not the best meal we've had, though filling none the less. We still had some cheese and we ate it sparingly, we had to make it last. We never knew when we would have another meal.

Meagan was in terrible shape now; she

was tired and sick all the time it seemed, with her being almost eight moons, I guess it can be expected. Tia was losing weight and was very thin by now, she wasn't being her normal bubbly self anymore. Morgan stayed strong and tried to hunt when he could, though he was just as hungry and tired as the rest of us. I was not as worried about myself as I was the rest. I was not a big eater before we started this venture anyhow. I am sure that I will be fine until we make it to the village Morgan talks about.

The storm had now been raging for two weeks and we did not seem to be getting any closer to this village of rest. We have not seen trees for four days now.

Chapter 16

"After the storm"

After seventeen days and nights the storm slowly subsided. We were tired, wet and very hungry. We have already eaten almost all of our cheese. At least we were able to share it equally between us. Even Meagan did not have more than anyone else. She was so sick to her stomach from all the raw meat, she really could not stomach the cheese that well either.

We were able to find a water hole with a few downed trees in the light of day, Oh sun light, how we have missed it! We cleaned up and washed our clothing; we drank clean cool water and slept until we had no choice but to look for food. I chose to look for any eatable plant life. Tia started a fire and hung our clothing and bedrolls in the trees to dry. Morgan took king to look for any small wild life to cook. I had very little luck finding much plant life. The rain had washed most of it away, or killed it. We were in a muddy grassy land with few other plants. There were not many trees either. Now, that we could see farther than our hand in front of our face, it seemed to be mostly grass.

We were in the same location recuperating for three days. Meagan was feeling better, though not much. The small child she carried was causing her many aches. She believed that she would have her daughter before we reached her home. I assured her, that in my dreams, she was still with child when we reached the island. It did not make her feel better. She was still sore and weak. Tia was most thin, her cloak and gown hung on her as it did the tree. Morgan was worried about his betrothed, and wondered if he was a father yet. He was in a hurry to reach home, though he was no less kind and patient to us and his sister. He was a very kind and gentle man, I would be proud to call him brother. I was worried about Meagan and her child, as weak as Meagan was. I decided on our third night, at these trees, to cast a healing bubble for us all. I worried that it would drain me, if it even worked in my weakened state.

I cast the protection bubble and once it was strong, I asked the Goddess Brighid for the strength and the power to heal us all and ready us for travel in the morning light. We all slept well and I knew we were protected from the wild. I did not dream this night as I have not dreamt for the whole storm. I was glad, as I woke with the dawning light. I sat and watched the bubble of purple dissipate with the light, I wondered why it was only able to form in the dark, and then I figured that we do not glow in the light either. It must be the only way this magic works.

Chapter 17

"The village of rest"

As the day arrived, and the sun rose, we all awoke feeling energized and ready to make this trip. We gathered our things and started out. We did not even feel the need for food at this time. It must have been because of the healing I asked Brighid for that has made us so well.

We traveled as before, we stopped when the sun was high in the sky. We had a fire and rabbit. We drank water we had collected. We have not really said much to one another since the storm started. I guess we have just gotten used to not speaking, just going through the motions. Unpack our things, start the fire, or try to make a shelter. Morgan and king were hunting, and we ladies rested until the food was ready to eat. However this time we ate, packed up our things and put out the fire. We started back to our journey at once. We have not found the village yet, though Morgan says it must be close. We were close when the storm started. I was a little afraid that we were lost, and going the wrong way. We were seeing birds flying through the air and small animals scurrying around looking for food and clean water. We all were at peace with the world the way it was, and glad it was not raining, this is certain! Meagan was so much better after the healing bubble that she walked with renewed energy and strength. It was as if she was her old self. Tia and Morgan walked together for a while and just looked out at the world. They really were a lot alike. They both love animals and children. They seemed also to be racing each other to see who could walk the farthest, and the fastest. Meagan was getting a kick out of watching them. I was, As I said, worried. I did not bother to say much about it. My dreams foretold that we would make it safely. The storm that had destroyed parts of the island village, in my dreams, which we were traveling to, had already occurred, I hoped. I felt we would be all right, so I did not worry anyone else with my depressing thoughts. Sure, I should say something; though Morgan was from this island, we were looking for. He would be the one to know which way to go. We were still heading in the same direction as when we left the forest.

We traveled on for two more days, when we saw the village on the horizon. We were so excited that we did not even bother to stop for a break in the midday that day. Morgan and Tia were almost running. I walked with Meagan, whom had started feeling very much with child by now, and walked in a different fashion now as well. She was tired, and I could tell she wanted to stop, though she wanted to get to the village more. Now that she was eight moons along, she was getting excited to see and hold her little one. I knew that Meagan was a strong and able woman, though I knew she could not run like Tia and Morgan, and so did she.

Morgan and Tia slowed down and waited for us when they got too far ahead. We were making good time now. I requested we stop. I faked that I was too tired to go on. I knew that Meagan needed to rest, no matter how much in a hurry that she was. We all wanted to get to the village, but we did not need Meagan getting ill from the heat and the sun. Therefore, we stopped under a single tree that had a great shade. There were nuts on the ground. We had quite a delicious snack with our rest. We only stopped long enough to catch breath we then started out again. We could see the village now, though there did not seem to be anyone there.

We reached the village after dark, there were fires going, however we still saw no people. We walked from hut to hut finding no one. We stopped and took advantage of a large fire in the center of the village. After a couple of hours, a small girl of about ten came wandering by us. She seemed to be in a hurry. Morgan said he would return, and followed her. Meagan said, "These people are kind, though they are shy. They must be in hiding until we leave or they know we are kind people. I cannot imagine why the young girl revealed herself, with no one else around."

I wondered aloud, "I feel as though no one is here. Not even the little girl. Maybe it is the same as on the island. I could not feel them either. I wonder if these people are related to them."

Meagan and Tia said, "What?"

I finally revealed my dreams, in complete. I also told them "I have been feeling all day as though we were going the wrong way. I cannot explain this, though I feel this cannot be real. I feel as though this village is more like a dream, or a mirage. Like its, well, not real."

Meagan thought about my story and

comments for a while, Then said, "It has been known to slip out of time to another place. It is possible when you cast your healing spells we slipped out of time and we are in a village from long ago, that is not here anymore. Our village has spells protecting it from outsiders, so maybe this village does too."

I contemplated this idea for a few. "I don't feel that we slid thru time. More like we are still in our time, the village is what moved."

Meagan said, "I guess it's probable. If a person can slip, then maybe a village can too. I cannot feel anyone either. You may be correct. How do you propose that it occurred?"

Tia said, "Melinda's Magic is raw and uncontrolled. If Melinda is as powerful as your grandmother, Or even more powerful, then she might have brought the village through time to help us to heal. It seems to be here, only the people seem to be displaced."

Morgan returned with the child and said, "This is Maya Retued. She says that she is eight years old. There does not seem to be any more people here. I had to look hard enough to find her, that if there were someone else I would have seen them. Why do you think this child is all alone here? And Meagan, doesn't her name seem familiar?" Maya went to look after the fire and let us talk.

Meagan talked to Morgan and explained our discussion. "We feel that this village has slipped through time, to give us a village of rest and recuperation. Melinda cannot control her powers yet, so we believe that during the healing spell she must have thought about a village, one we would be safe in until we could get to the village you spoke of before the storm."

Morgan said, "Is this possible? I have heard of people slipping, though not villages, with or without people. Why is Maya here? I thought it was unbelievable that she has our mother's name. What do you think of that?"

Meagan looked from me to Tia, "She does have our mother's name. I believe this to be true; I believe this village is from the past. Our mother must have been from here. I never knew this. Maybe this is why the village slipped through at this time. We needed it and our mother knew we would, not for visions, because she was here. She might have figured out a way to help us, from the past. I feel tired and need to rest, and so do the rest of you. I do not know how long this village will remain. We must retire and talk in the morning."

We all agreed and went into the nearest hut, the child ran away to the next one, Morgan slept outside to keep watch. King stayed at his side.

CHAPTER 18

"Lost in time"

When we awoke, the village was busting with people. We must have slipped back in time with the village. It looked like any village that would be here today, though these people did not look like Morgan and Meagan, and me for that matter. They were taller and did not have the same pointed ears, pointed chin, slanted green eyes, or pail skin that we had. They looked more like Tia's people.

We were still in the grassland, and the huts were made of grass and mud instead of sticks, leaves and mud. Everyone was so busy.

There seemed to be some kind of festival or ceremony about to be underway. Some of the villagers were in costumes and others were selling goods on the street. Others were busy doing Dailey activities; I guess we all must work sometimes. We wandered out of the huts and soon found the center of the village cluttered with people and items for sale or trade. We browsed the items and found a few items that we might be able to use in our continued journey.

I was worried that we would be here for a short while. However, we all could use the rest. Is that not what I asked the goddess' Brighid for after all? We just went with the flow of things and enjoyed our stay. We ate when we were hungry and rested when we got tired. We used the huts we awoke in; they did not seem to belong to anyone anyway.

We worked to help the villagers for payment in items and coin when we could. The villagers did not seem to notice that we were not from their village. They treated us as though we belonged.

We did not really keep track of time while we were there; we figured that we had to live our lives that we have been given, for however long it lasted. We were getting eager for our travel to continue, even if we would be miserable again, and alone.

Morgan had found everyday work with a group of men who showed how to sharpen their hunting tools to other men. The festivities seemed to be an everyday occurrence. Tia joined up with a group of young women who cared for the village children. They taught the children in groups according to their age. They taught them sewing, fishing, hide tanning, gardening etc. Meagan was under the care of the village Shaman, She was a Wiccan mage, who doctored the village. She called herself a midwife, I had never heard of a midwife. Meagan was being taught how to be a mother and a midwife. I learned for the first time that Meagan's Betrothed husband had perished before she knew she was with child. She was in hiding in a remote location near her cottage with Morgan's wife and their mothers... They were hiding because of a group of outsiders who had raided the village and killed many of their men, and took many of the women who were young enough to bear children. She was in hiding when she fell ill and Morgan took her to the foothill forest. Meagan was interested in medicine and healing magic. She felt that she would need to know these traits when she returned to their village. A lot of healing is sure to be needed.

I was told by the mage that I was a great sorceress, and could wield some great magic. I could in fact wield any type of magic that I wanted to. I chose the healing magic only because I am familiar with healing. I was studying other types of magic as well. This mage was familiar with the magic that I have already managed to produce, so she was more than willing to teach me how to control it.

My Leopard was not feared in this village and was welcomed by most into their huts and stores. Many of the villagers fed King as though he were theirs. I was glad, though he wandered around the village and was hardly at my side.

I helped to make medicine, salves, and bottled herbs for the shaman or mage if you like. She was so impressed with my work that she wanted me to stay on; I had to explain to her our situation.

Our story was not so unusual to the Mage. She said that she could help to get us back into our own time any time we liked. Meagan said that she wanted to learn more before we left. Morgan said that was fine with him, he wanted to earn some more coins before we left, and he wanted to gather some more supplies as well. Tia was defiantly enjoying the teaching, and said she was with me and would stay as long as we wanted to.

I was wondering if there was a spell on us to make us want to stay. I asked the mage if it were possible. "Melinda, how do you feel that you four happened to arrive in this village? Could it be that you all had some things to learn before your journey continued?" The mage asked. I said, "It is indeed possible, though I always have felt that it had to do with my healing spell. Maybe the gods' and goddesses' took me too seriously." This led the Mage to look through her magic books passed down over 1000 years. She would let me know if she found anything.

I looked for the child with the name "Maya" every day that we were there, No one could ever tell me where she was. I thought that I would try it. It was getting dark out and I had little time left to find her today, I would have to search tomorrow.

When we awoke, I had a feeling that today would be our last here. The mage had told me she could help us return to our own time when we felt ready. I searched for Maya for a good part of the morning hours. I was heading back to the mages hut, when Maya walked past me and went into the mages hut. I was in shock, I guess ask and you shall receive. Meagan was there and sat to talk to little Maya. I walked in and sat with them. Maya had an odd story for us.

Chapter 19

"Maya's Story"

Maya started, "I have been taught since I was brought into this world, that I would someday meet four travelers. I did not know when I would meet them. I am only guessing that you four are the travelers I was to meet. I have been taught that I would help these travelers to complete their journey. I have come here to my mother's hut to speak with you, Meagan and Melinda. My mother does not know that I have been taught of your travels. I felt your group was the foretold travelers when all my people vanished, which left me all alone here. For hours, I tried to figure it out and when I saw your group of four travelers enter our village, I felt it was right. I need to help you get along with your journey and I need all of you together so I can speak to you all. Melinda, would you get Morgan and Tia, and meet Meagan and myself at the hut you have been sleeping in?"

I agreed to find Tia and Morgan and return to the hut. Morgan pled with me to wait, I said, "We cannot wait, Finish and arrive in an hour at our hut." Morgan halfheartedly agreed. I located Tia with her group of children at the creek where she was teaching a group of young men to fish. Tia wrapped up her teaching and walked the children back into the village. We walked together to the hut. We were all present except for Morgan. Meagan went to find him and tried to talk him into returning. He was being stubborn until she mentioned his wife and child. Then he seemed to snap out of whatever possessed him to stay. He brought King with him and joined us at the hut. It was going to be dark within the next few hours and I felt it was urgent to get this done as soon as little Maya could accomplish it.

Maya repeated her story for Morgan and Tia. "Now I need to get my mother and we will return you to your time." Morgan said he would return in a few minutes, he needed to get some supplies, and a horse. Tia found a small wagon and asked to purchase it; the wagon was not for sale. Maya talked the owner in to lending it to us. She said she would explain all to the owner as soon as we slipped back to our own time.

Maya and Morrigan her mother, Who indeed had the same names as Meagan and Morgan's mother and grandmother, joined us and burned some herbs and said a spell. As we sat in a circle holding hands, we noticed that the villagers seemed to disappear, slowly one at a time. They simply faded away. I was feeling dizzy. I started chanting, a golden glow surrounded us, and we all fell into sleep.

When I awoke, Maya was still with us, although the village and villagers were gone. Maya was awake and had built a fire. I was astounded. I said, "Maya how are we to get you back to your own time?"

Maya said, "I will be able to leave once you have completed your great journey. I am destined to be here with you at this time. I was groomed from birth to help you in this journey. You are why I am here. You need guidance; I will provide what I can."

Morgan, Tia, and Meagan were still

sleeping and the golden circle still shimmered softly around us. I asked, "Did I cast this circle? Am I the one who brought us here?" Maya said, "Yes, it is said that you are the greatest sorceress born to our clan ever. You will help to defend and protect the island in the future. The village that you conjured was here long ago, and I was born there. I know of the place you journey to and I must say to you, you will bring it out of darkness when it matters most." She paused and looked into my eyes, then said, "You will meet me at the Inn." I asked her, "What do you mean? I have already met you." She replied, "You will know when the time is right. Now, get some rest. We must travel early to get you to the island."

Chapter 20

"My dreams come true"

We awoke and traveled in the dark before morning came. I was glowing faintly as did Morgan, Meagan, and Maya. We together lit a circle around us and we were able to see some distance in the dark. We walked for a couple of hours when the sky began to light on the horizon. Maya stopped and looked into the fading darkness behind us. I heard the strange flapping noises again, and turned around. What I saw was a set of glowing red eyes. That is all I saw. Maya slowly approached the eyes that seemed to float near us. Morgan tried to stay her. She slowly kept walking. Meagan was not frightened, though she had had a start. Tia was white as a spirit. I kept hearing the flapping noises and thought it rather sounded like a humming birds wings. Maya led the eyes closer to us. As the sun rose, slowly we began to see a shape appearing, attached to the floating red glowing eyes. Tia walked backwards slowly and Morgan and Meagan stood still. Maya asked me to walk to her side. She said, "This is a green forest dragon. He seems to have followed you from your forest. Speak to him. He is here for you alone."

I approached the forest dragon and spoke softly to him. I asked him his name. However, I suddenly knew it already. "O'Mear", I said. "How did you find me so far from home?" Morgan and Meagan talked quietly to each other. Tia was in need of a seat.

I spoke to O'Mear some more and he flew straight up into the air above me. I said, "Maya, I think he had a hard time finding me while we were in your village for so long. He seemed worried. How do I know his name and other thoughts?" Maya said, "He seems to be your dragon from the past. When you were a small child, you were lost to the forest and he took you under his wing, so to speak. He insured that you found a home and watched over you since then." "For thirty years, that's amazing. Why have I not seen or heard him before?" I asked. Maya said, "He was there for you and you alone. Had you needed him he would have shown himself to you sooner. He will remain with you until he passes on." I was thrilled; I did not know much of my life before Hill Dale village. I seemed to be getting it all in pieces, from different sources. I asked, "O'Mear, Can you allow Meagan to ride you to the Island? She is too far with child now to walk with much speed." O'Mear silently agreed and lowered down for Meagan to sit on his back.

We walked and O'Mear flew Meagan behind us. We were making great time I felt. Morgan said the village he referred to, that is next to the ocean, was up ahead. Meagan and O'Mear flew on ahead and she was resting next to the water when we arrived two hours later. She was already due to have her little one, and she tired. We found her a place to nap, while we arranged a boat to take us to the island in the morning. Tia, Meagan, and Morgan were sleeping when Maya came to speak to me that night. Maya told me, "You must fly ahead on the dragon to the island. You must see that the island is safe for Meagan's arrival in the morning. She will be birthing a very special daughter and we must insure her safety."

I asked, "How do you know this? Must I leave now, or can I rest first? If the island is not safe then how do I make it so?"

Maya said, "You have too many questions. You can rest, though you must go tonight. If the island has outsiders on it, your dragon will help you to wield a strong magic to erase them from sight. That is what dragons are best for. They help you to make your magic stronger. You are lucky to have a green forest dragon. Most great mages are taught from birth how to wield their magic. You were not. You will need his help and he knows how to help you. He knows your thoughts and you know his. You will know what to do when the time comes."

I rested and ate some wild boar. I fed my

dragon some hay from the stable area where we left the horse and wagon. I felt as though I was in for a wild ride tonight. First of all, I have never flown. Second of all, I have been waiting to see this island for many, many moons now. This was nothing like my dreams. However, the dreams had me standing on a shore with Tia, Meagan, and Morgan. Maya was not there nor was my dragon O'Mear. I guess that I was just not seeing them there in my dreams. I did not know of Maya or O'Mear at the time I had my dreams. However, I guess that they would have to be there if it were a futuristic dream.

As the moon raised high in the sky, I took flight on O'Mear. We went to the island and flew over it as high as we could to have a look around. It was the island from my dreams, now it was coming true. I did in fact know the whole island. I was also able to tell when I saw the outsiders. I knew they were not from this island. O'Mear and I glowed very bright from my magic. The outsiders were throwing spears at us and they were lit up by fire. I chanted a spell from a different language and fire seemed to shoot from the sky, and suddenly the outsiders all disappeared. The flames enveloped them and took them away. I have no idea how this happened. I did not feel as though I did anything. I was not drained at all as I feel like I should have been. By the time we had found and erased all of the outsiders, three groups in all, it was already becoming morning. We flew to the shore where the boat would dock with the rest of our party.

Chapter 21

"The Inn"

We silently waited for the boat to arrive for close to three hours when I decided to start a small fire. Just then, O'Mear flew off into the air. I saw him fly to the area that, we had been to when; we found the last group of outsiders. The Sky was clear and the air was crisp. I awaited the boat and my dragons return.

After the day drew close to time for mid-day meal, the boat finally arrived. Tia, Morgan, Meagan and young Maya un-boarded the boat. We unloaded our belongings and sat at the fire. Maya went to see the area where the last group of outsiders was erased from. We stood and looked over the ocean. It was exactly like my first dream. King was behind me as we turned around and walked to the east, also just like my dream. I tried to hear O'Mear as we searched for Maya. I felt no one except for Tia, also like the dream. I stopped when we could see the Inn. I felt the urge to go to it this time. I could feel the dew on the tall grass and the stone wall was sweating. I reached the door and read the sign aloud. Meagan was surprised. She said, "You can read ancient Celtic writing?" I said, "Yes, it appears so. I first saw it in my dream and had to see if it was really here." I pushed open the heavy oak door and we walked in. As I looked at the logbook, Meagan and Morgan walked through the door across from the entrance. I looked around down stairs and Tia went up the stairs to look around. As I passed the door opposite the entrance I saw the bright flash of light and heard the loud ear-piercing scream at the same time, this time it was real and I did not wake up. I flew through the door and found Morgan standing over Meagan, who was birthing her daughter. I was astounded when I saw the baby for the first time. She was smaller than she should have been, but this was not what shocked me. She had wings and pointed ears. She was just like a faerie. I did not know what to think. Morgan handed me the baby and went to light a fire in the wall made of stone. The smoke I feared was going to be too much for Meagan and her daughter. I found out that the fire's smoke rose through the ceiling and into the sky. Tia ran down the stairs to see what was wrong, I showed her Meagan's baby. She was in awe!

Meagan had passed out from the pain,

and when she came to, we handed her daughter to her. She started crying, she too was surprised to find out her child had wings. Maya was in the doorway when I turned to exit the room. Maya said, "Meagan fear not. Your child, Marinna, is a special girl who will bring the Fae and your people together. There will no longer be any reason to live separate from your kin and theirs. This island will be a true magical island where all can live as one. Your daughter will lead the Fae back home and they will wander no longer in search of a place to belong. Melinda will help in her teachings. She will know all of her family, yours and the Fae. She will live here always, and never want for anything. Now it is time for you to heal and continue home. I must leave you now. I will return to my own time, so that I may see you later." Maya slowly faded and was here no longer.

Chapter 22

"Home, Sweet home"

Meagan was in deep thought as we walked out of this Inn. Tia was no longer scared. She felt like she belonged here as well. I told her that we must return her to Hill dale once we get to Maya's home and Meagan is settled with her little one. Morgan was indeed in a hurry to get home to his wife, child, and mother.

We continued to the east only a short walk. Meagan took the lead and walked up to the door of the hut. Meagan knocked on the door. A mid aged woman with long blond hair down to her ankles opened the door. She was wearing a white house gown and a white fuzzy cloak. My dream was true. Meagan introduced Tia and me. Maya just answered, "I know". I stepped into her arms and she told me she had waited a lifetime to meet me again. I cried. I could no longer hold it in, and I cried. Meagan and Morgan went into the room past us. Morgan walked up to a door and softly knocked. A woman, Merida, with light red blond hair opened the door. She held a baby in her arms. You have a son and she named him Matthew. She fell into his arms and wept quietly. Tia watched the reunion and cried silently herself. She cried for the happiness that surrounded her. Meagan took a seat in a rather large cotton plant stuffed; well she called it a chair, what an odd chair. I clung to Maya and asked her, "Am I home? Are you my mother? Am I finally home? Please tell me…" Maya answered, "Yes, you are my child from long ago lost. I searched for days for you. I went in search for food and wood for a fire. You must have wandered off. Where did you go?" I told her the story that my grandmother Rose had told, and asked her, "Why were you in the forest so far from your home, this island?" She answered, "I was looking for the village of Hill Dale, and I searched for three young women, your Tia here, Meagan and yourself it would seem, as well as one young man, apparently Morgan. As well and a man named Morgan. I knew of the journey, you see, from birth I was told to wait for the four travelers. I remembered helping four travelers when I was so young, only eight. I knew the names of the four woodlanders and had remembered the village you were from. I wanted to get the journey over with. I thought that if I went to Hill dale and found you four, that I could explain the journeys importance and get it under way. I was foolish and did not realize you three were my children in reality." I said, "Not foolish, just eager. But if you had already met us in your village of birth and already helped us back then, why go looking for us later, when you got older?" Maya said, "Because of all the troubles we were having with the outsiders at that time. I knew what you, Melinda, and your dragon had done to erase them before, well in the here and now, while I was here when I was eight... It gets so confusing. I needed your help thirty years ago, just as we did today. It is so hard to put into words being that I have slipped through time a few times and it is all in my memories from long ago. Even though it only just happened for you."

We sat and chatted among each other for

quite a while. We held the babies and spoke of the future. Maya, my newfound mother, was happy we were all home. Tia was in no big hurry to leave. She said, "We have only just arrived here and I think I want to stay for a while. I would like to remain on this island and make a home. It is so nice here and I feel my teaching skills might be well needed in the future, if not now. Melinda can help me start a magic school and we can get the Fae to return here for a visit and see if they like it. I know that Marinna will be the one to make it happen, but I might be needed until then at least."

Dear Diary,

I AM FINALLY HOME!

Melinda Fairling,

(Now of Mystic Island, Ireland!)

Biography:

Susan Christine Slater is thirty-three and lives in Livingston Texas with her husband and three children. Melinda Fairling has become a family name in the Slater household and this is the first of many books to come. Hope you enjoy them all!

New Book

Coming in 2010:

Wicca on a full Moon :

Book 2 –

Life on Mystic Island

Chapter 1

"Catching up..."

I have been home for three years now. I know that I am truly happy when I wake to see my eyes so bright, even in the daytime. I feel that it is all going so well. It is unbelievably wonderful to be back home! It feels great to see myself in the faces of others! To know that I have a family. I have met many new people and I adore them all! Everyone is just like me now that we are on Mystic Island! My life ambitions are the same as my fellow villagers now as well.

Everyone comes to me for help
doing things around the island. They ask for
spells and potions, to heal and cure, and for love
and protection, I love it. I feel so needed, even
though I have not found that "one true calling"
of mine own yet. I know that I will settle down
and choose my path as soon as I learn more
about magic and my village islands ways. As for
now, I really just help where I am needed, Just
for now.

       This is how it has been since we
arrived on our island soon after the storm. We
had to rebuild, more than we could repair,
during the clean up. Everyone just helped
everyone else. Everyone has been so kind, and
willing to help each other out wherever they can.
I need to tell you, I really want

nothing more than to teach others and to keep our magic alive. I think that teaching will end up being what I choose to do for my life's path. I have been learning different types of magic so that I can be a good teacher, and so that I can protect this island when need be. Magic is helpful in so many ways that you can not Even imagine. Here are just a few things I can tell you about magic; You can cast spells to help plants grow, cast protection bubbles, travel through time and from place to place on the astral plains. There are Magical rituals for every season, and every activity you can think of. I can levitate, see glowing auras, and meditate. In addition, when I cast circles correctly, I can see a bright shimmering light where I envision my circles to be. I can glow in the dark, and so do my Eyes.

my eyes glow most of the time now, non-stop!
Even during the day time hours! Especially
when I am casting spells and other magic. I am
more powerful than most of the other villagers,
though. There is a spell tying down this village
to using names that only begin with the letter
"M". I feel that I can break the spell that this
village is under if I only try to find a way. Only
our people who have names that begin with the
letter "M" have magic powers. Therefore, you
see, the spell has to be broken soon. The fact
is I have to try something! It is not normal to be
without powers, as some of our people are. We
will soon have to find another way to keep our
magic going without names that begin with the
letter "M".

my magic seems to have gone into hiding

when I really want to use it the most, though. I have found out that it is easier to wield magic when I did not really plan it out, as if it just flows through me instead of from me. If I think about it, too much before hand it does not work, as I want it to, if it works at all.

Over the three years that I have been home, I have tried so hard to get used to not sensing the other people around me. I still have a hard time with this, I get startled a lot. People seem to just "pop" in from nowhere. I do startle easy now! I used to be able to sense everyone around me in the foothill forest. It seems the only people I can sense now are the fae folk, sometimes, and Tia, my oldest and best friend ever.

Now... I believe that if the fae are to

one-day return to this magical, mystical island, there is a lot still to be done. We have started building relations with the Fae folk and I hope it will be a great and wonderful year indeed. We have received help from a few wayward fae who have wondered onto our island of mystical paradise. They seem unafraid of us and are glad to help us better understand their people and their ways of life. They teach us what the fae expect from others around them. These fae are grateful that we want to return the fae to this beautiful place. They teach us their magical ways, about time travel as well as air and water spells, in the hope that one day their people will return to their ancestral home.

Tia, my best friend in the land is still by my side in all of this. She remained here with me after our long tedious travels. She is also learning so much more about magic than she knew before we came here. She is glad to have the fae teachers, as well as my people to help her with her learning's.

My mom, Maya has sent word to the fae to join us in a convention to discus their return for the future. We will have a festival of sorts with games, music, shows, and food. Any fae who show up for the convention and festivities will be lodged in the new buildings we have constructed just for them. The Fae live in Kind of a beehive, only bigger. A hut in a tree with many rooms. The Fae are neat and tidy persons. The homes we have made are for temporary purposes. If any Fae wish to remain on the island after the fall they will be allowed to build their homes any place on the island that they wish. I have Learned that the fae are particular of their surroundings and most are not very trusting towards the non-flying types of persons. They love their own group of Fae to be around them at all times. If one travels too far away from their group, the others get highly worried, agitated, almost frightened. I have now met and worked with many fae folk. I feel that I am starting to understand them quite well, though there is still a lot to learn.

Tia is quite an adventurer, and well versed in our villages' ancestry already, quite remarkably for the short time we have been here. Tia stays on our island and never goes far from me, though she is usually searching and digging and reading all she can. She teaches our pre

adults to learn the ways of our ancestors. She
does very well. She teaches some about
horticulture and Wiccan medicines. However,
hunting, fishing, sewing, hide tanning and baking
are all her specialties'. she teaches an array of
different subjects to her students. Its not all
about magic, though she does teach a fair
amount of spells and incantations! She is
learning a lot from the students as well. One
day one student, Marcus, Found a Stone
structure that was buried by the North shore of
the island. Marcus explained that his mother's
father had told stories of a village long ago lost
on the north side of the island. Tia spent all
afternoon with Marcus and his family hearing
all the stories about this "lost village".

Although, I am worried for Tia just now,

she has a secret she will not or can not share

with me yet, and this is bothersome to me. I know

we all have the right to our secrets, but I cannot

ever feel what hers' is all about. I used to be able

to read her better. I guess I will just have to wait

until she is ready to confide in me. I worry that

She secretly wants to leave for her home soon

and I worry we will not be able to magically or

physically protect our selves. We are learning,

just slowly. I really do not know how we were so

lucky to have gotten here without meeting up

with other persons or the outsiders' and any real

problems arising. We were definatly lucky on

our trip here. The storm was hard and difficult

for our journey, though we never met with life

threatening danger, other than hunger.

my Dragon, "O'Meara" is a very helpful

and quite a comical creature. He flies around our village island and brings me things. Lots of things! He tells me that I need them. However, I know not what for. I have all the items stored in a small hut behind my moms' house. She wishes I would sort them out! Nevertheless, how can I twiddle down the pile and still have what I might need? I have not needed any of these particular items as of yet, though I do keep them. Just in case. He knows things I cannot see or feel yet. He knows things of the future and the past, even places he has never been before. We communicate regularly though he doesn't ever tell me what I need these objects for. I have learned quite a lot from him. We fly almost daily, although not just for fun, we must do regular sweeps of the island to ensure my peoples

safety from the outsiders' and other dangers.
We have only encountered a few outsiders' and
were able to "Erase" them without a problem.

Meagan has been busy with her awesome
little girl Marinna. When the village elders heard
about Meagan's newborn daughter, they felt a
new prophecy was unfolding before our own
eyes. I learned when Marinna was born that she
would be the one to bring the Fae back to this
island. And I hope this is true, I would love
nothing more than to see the fae return to this
magical place. After all, it was their home first.

Marinna Learned to fly before she
learned to walk. This is all new to us. The Fae
folk are really a great help when it comes to her
teachings. She doesn't walk much even now that
she knows how, and she is hard to catch when

you need to get her out of things. Meagan really does have her hands full! As do we all, when we are rotating watch over the wee one. Marinna is busier than any three year old on the island, or not on the island for that matter. She is smaller than all children her age and is hard to keep your eye on, being smaller and being able to fly makes it quite a chore.

Meagan has met a new love, named Melvyn, and will be wed in three turns of the full moon . Full moons are lucky for us Wiccan's, in case you never heard. I still don't understand why yet, though. I never learned about all the different moons until we came here. I am learning slowly and a lot of things at once. We are all so happy for Meagan and Melvyn and we wish them only the best.

Morgan and his wife, Merida have
another wee one on the way, we are hoping for a
boy this time too. She is twice the size of her
moons along, only 4 moons along and already
the size she was when she had Matthew! We
worry for her, although she is not unhappy. We
just help her when we can and make her do a fair
amount of resting. Morgan is fretful at times.
We all see him as quite a nervous father and
husband! He says that he isn't a great hunter or
a farmer. He has no real skills that he
perseveres at. Though he can do many things,
and he can do them well, he still worries he will
not be able to raise his family well. He wonders
how he is to feed his brood if they have many
more. I understand his pain, he radiates from the
stress. Poor Morgan, my dear brother. I love

him, so I try to help him anyway I can, and when I can. I have had O'Meara hunt for him at times, though Morgan doesn't know it was my idea. King, my leopard, goes hunting when Morgan goes. I think that he feels like Morgan needs help, so he goes with him. I feel for Morgan, though I am really quite too busy just now to help much. With all the learning and the teaching, I don't really have time for myself either.

I haven't yet been off this island since we travelled from the Foothill forest, though I haven't had the urge to leave for anything either. It is such a great island. I can hardly believe I was born here. I only wish my father were here to share in my new found home, life, and abilities. I want so much for him to return, though Maya says it's not realistic to believe that he's still out there. She gave up on seeing me again a long time ago, too. Shall I find him on future travels? I hope so; it would complete me, to the fullest.

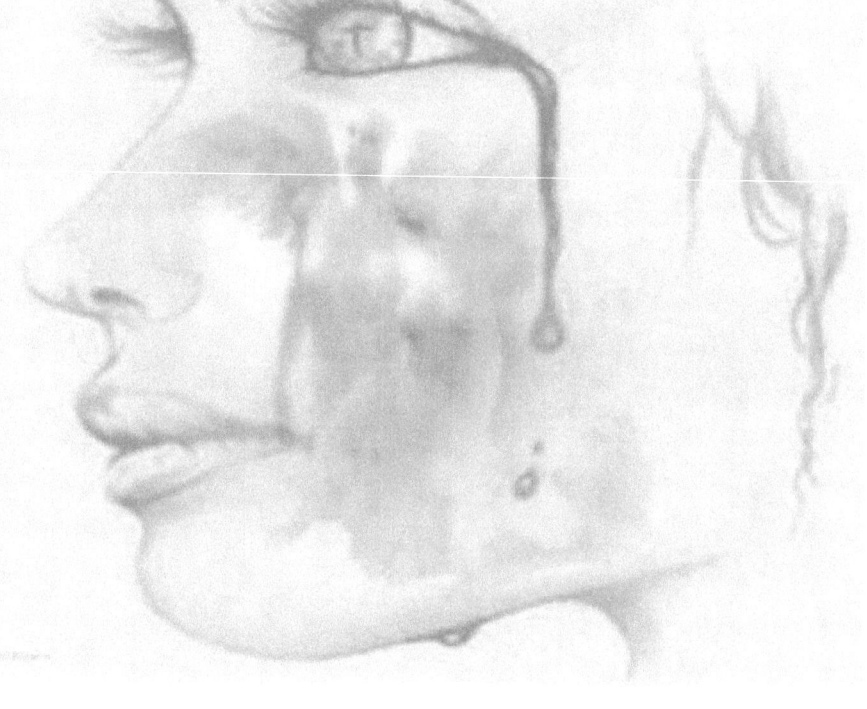

Look For My Newest Book Online

And In Stores June 2010

Wicca On A Full Moon:

Book 2- Life On Mystic Island